CONTENTS

OVERVIEW

Surfing has been around for many years. It is one of the most thrilling sports on the planet.

Kelly Slater

Lifestyle

Surfing is much more than a healthy, fun sport. Surfing can become a way of life.

SURFING

John Allan

www.hungrytomato.com

First published in 2022 by Hungry Tomato Ltd.
F1, Old Bakery Studios, Blewetts Wharf, Malpas Road, Truro, Cornwall, TR1 1QH, UK

ISBN 978 1 912108 29 9

A CIP catalogue record for this book is available from the British Library.

Printed in China.

Picture credits (t=top; b=bottom; c=center; l=left; r=right):

ACM Writing Group: 5t, 8, 11bl, 20, 29cr, 29b, 32, 33b. Simon Adams: 33t. Buzz Pictures/Alamy: 9b, 23t. Getty Images: 40, 41b. Tim Jones: 26, 38, 39t, 39b. Nordicphotos/Alamy: 22. O'Neill: 34/35t. Peterson: 7b. Quicksilver: 4, 5b. Shutterstock: 1, 3, 6t, 13 all, 24t, 28, 29t, 29cl, 46/47. Tracks: 44/45b. Tropicalpix: 36. Henrik Trygg/Corbis: 15cr. www.aspworldtour.com: 9t, 10/11t, 10b, 12, 14, 15t, 15cl, 15b, 16, 18/19t, 18b, 19bl, 19br, 23b, 25t, 25b, 27t, 27b, 31t, 31cr, 34b, 35b, 37, 41t, 41c, 42t, 42b, 43t, 43b. www.shortyphotos.com: 17t, 17b, 31cl, 31b. www.swillyphotos.com: 2, 11br, 30. www.hotstuffpictures.com: 21tr, 21cl.

Every effort has been made to trace copyright holders, and we apologise in advance for any omissions. We would be pleased to insert the appropriate acknowledgments in any subsequent edition of this publication.

Travel

Surfers travel long distances to surf, compete in competitions, and find the best waves.

Surfers are always trying to improve.

A surfer performs a fast turn on a wave

HISTORY OF SURFING

The Hawaiian people enjoyed surfing almost 1,000 years ago. When the first Europeans arrived in Hawaii in the late 1700s, surfing almost died out.

Then, just over 100 years ago, some old surfboards were found and surfing was rediscovered.

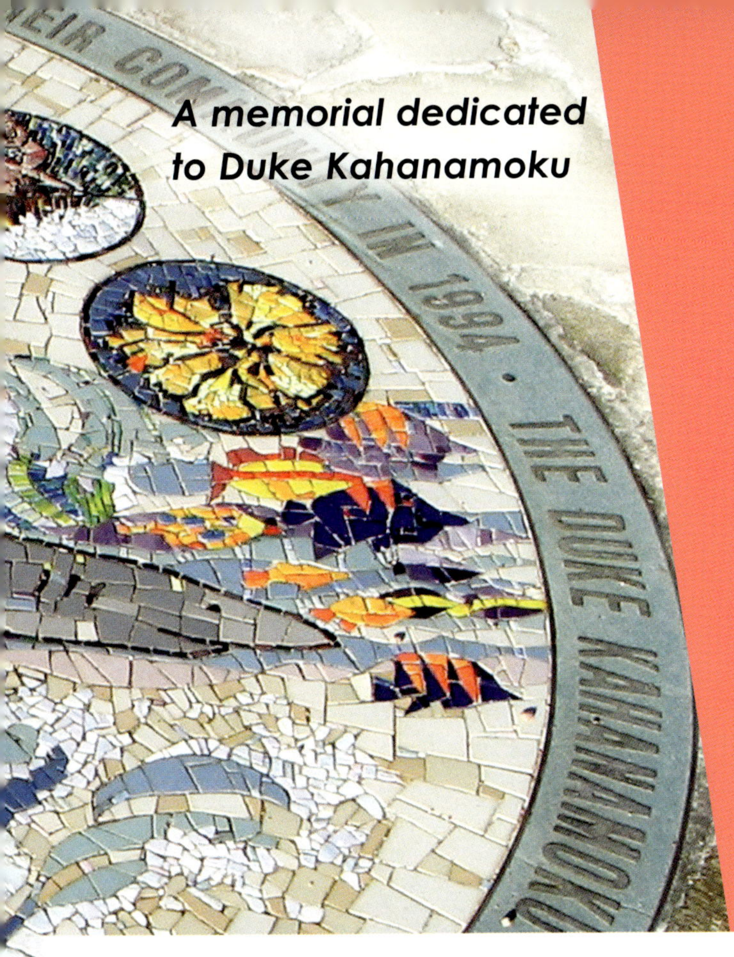

A memorial dedicated to Duke Kahanamoku

Travelling is a part of surfing

In the early 1900s, Olympic swimming champion, Duke Kahanamoku helped revive surfing in Hawaii.

1907 – George Freeth becomes the first surfer in California, USA.

1915 – Duke Kahanamoku introduces surfing to Australia.

1957 – Surfing is introduced in France by American, Peter Viertel.

1958 – One of the best waves in the world, Supertubes, is discovered in South Africa.

1961 – Australian, Peter Troy introduces surfing to Brazil.

1971 – Australian, Steve Cooney rides the 4.5 metres (15 feet) high Uluwatu wave in Bali, Indonesia.

TYPES OF SURFING

There are three main types of surfing: short boarding, long boarding and tow surfing.

A short-board surfer performs a perfect snap turn

Short boarding

Short boarding is the most common form of surfing. Short boarders perform a number of different turns on and above the waves. The boards are usually about 2 metres (6.5 feet) long.

Long boarding

In long boarding, the surfers let the waves direct them. The surfboards, sometimes called Malibus, are longer and heavier than short boards.

No need to paddle with tow surfing!

Tow surfing

Tow surfing involves surfers getting towed by a rope behind a jet ski.

Tow surfing is usually used for very large waves.

TYPES OF BOARD

The most popular board is the short board. But there are many different boards in all shapes and sizes.

A long board is thicker, heavier and more stable than a short board.

A long board is more difficult to turn. Long boards have a wide nose.

Surfers 'hang' their toes off the end

A fish is shorter than a short board but is much wider and thicker. A fish is designed for very small waves.

The fish is easy to paddle

A tow board is small but heavy

A tow board is towed into big waves by a powered craft. A tow board has feet straps.

ANATOMY OF A SURFBOARD

A surfboard can be broken down into four main parts: length, width, rails and fins.

Andy Irons inspects the damage done to the tail of his short board

Surfers call a group of surfboards a quiver.

Length

The length of the board is measured from the nose (front) of the surfboard to the tail (back).

Width

The width of the surfboard is measured at its widest point. This is usually halfway between the nose and tail.

Rails

The rails are the curved edges of the surfboard that run from the nose to the tail.

Fins

The fins at the back of the board make it stable. Surfboards can have between one and four fins. The most popular is three fins (a tri-fin).

EQUIPMENT

Besides a surfboard, surfers need other gear. This gear includes a wetsuit, leg rope and wax.

Sofia Mulanovich grew up surfing in Peru in cold water so she always wears a full-length wetsuit

Wetsuit

A wetsuit is a rubber suit that keeps surfers warm in cold water.

Leg rope

The leg rope is a cord that connects a surfer's leg to the board. This stops surfers losing their boards when they fall off.

Wax

Surfboards are made out of fibreglass. Wax is rubbed on to the surface of the board to provide grip, and prevent surfers from slipping off.

Deck grip

Deck grip

Deck grip is a pad that can be glued to a surfboard instead of using wax. It provides traction (grip).

BREAKING WAVES

Waves travel from way out in the deep ocean. They break when they reach shallower water.

How waves work

Waves break because the 'bottom' portion of the wave hits the shallow sand or reef.

The 'top' portion of the wave moves forward until the top portion falls over.

Flat sandy beaches that slope gently into the water have slow, low-rise waves

Wave speed

The faster a wave travels from deep to shallower water, the faster the wave breaks. In Hawaii, waves come from deep in the Pacific Ocean and break very fast on the shallow reefs.

A series of three waves break off the coast of Mexico

Sets

Waves usually arrive in groups called sets. Sets can be three, four or five waves that arrive one after the other.

Sets are normally bigger than other waves. Some sets can include up to ten waves!

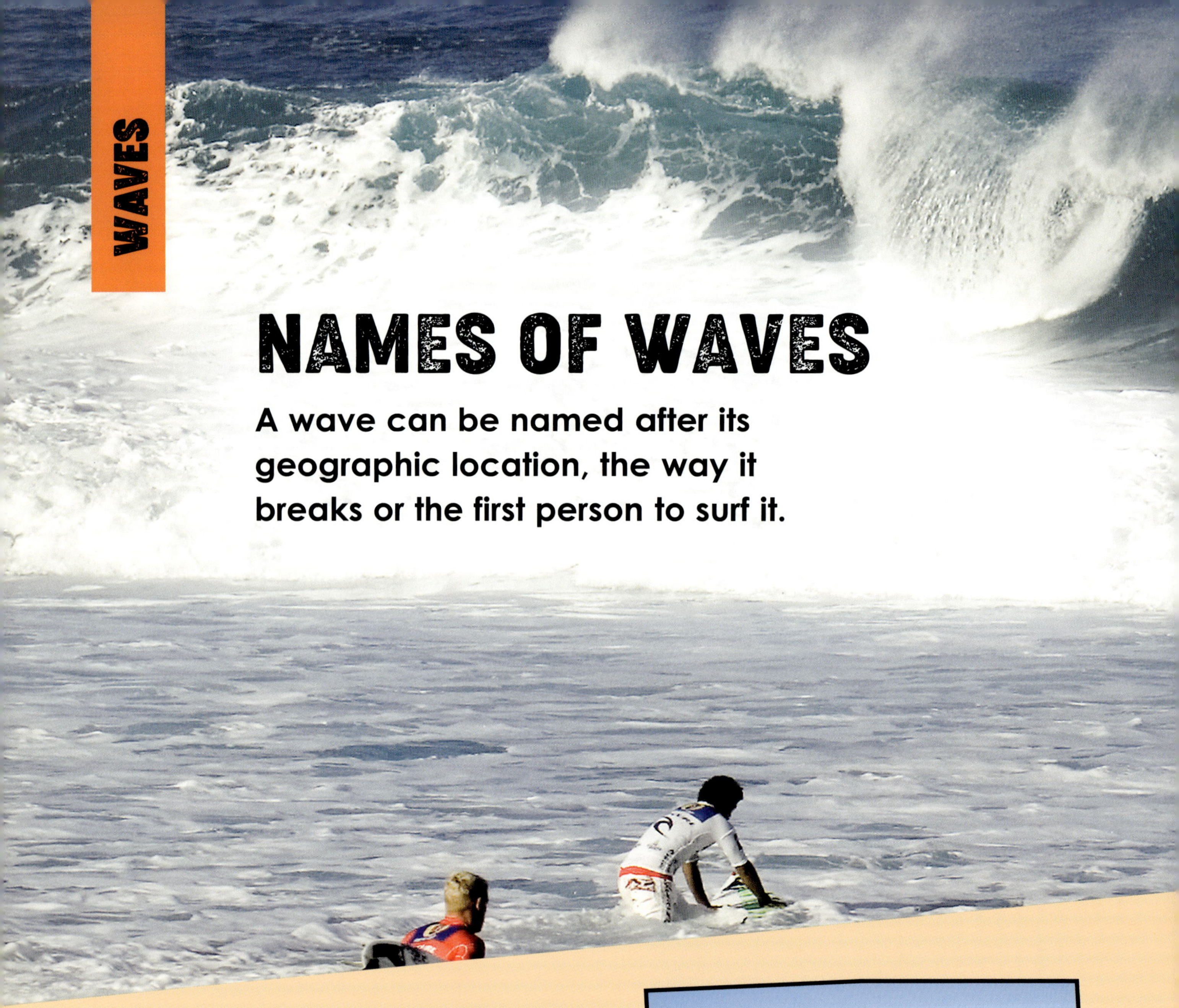

NAMES OF WAVES

A wave can be named after its geographic location, the way it breaks or the first person to surf it.

Beach Breaks are waves that break over a sandy beach. They are not forceful.

Beach Beaks can change from day to day as the sand moves.

Beach Break waves break in a random manner

Reef Breaks are waves that break over a reef or rock. They are powerful and can be dangerous.

The famous Hawaiian wave, Pipeline, breaking close to shore

Point Breaks are waves that wrap around a point or headland.

Waves roll down a sandy point break in Australia

THE BEST WAVES

Jeffreys Bay in South Africa is considered to have some of the best waves in the world

There are surfers riding waves all around the world. The waves that break the best, longest or biggest become famous and attract surfers.

In surfing, waves are said to break either left or right. A wave is called a right-hander if, from a surfer's viewpoint, it travels towards the right. A left-hander is the opposite.

Waves breaking on a coral reef off the coast of Fiji

In Hawaii, the waves are large and break in shallow water.

Australia has a wide range of waves.

In Indonesia, the waves break in perfect formation over coral reefs.

Australia has fun, small waves like this one, but it also has the towering Cyclops wave

SURFING THE WORLD

Surfers travel the globe searching for exciting new places to surf.

In August 2007, the world's first glacial surf ride on Copper River, Alaska, USA, was recorded.

Kealii Mamala and Garrett McNamara caught the waves when a large iceberg broke off from a glacier!

A surfer tackling the ice-cold Arctic waves off the coast of Norway

Wave freeze

New surfers thinking of travelling to Alaska or Iceland, beware! You'll need a thick wetsuit – the water there is only a few degrees above freezing.

Layne Beachley surfing Sunset Beach, Hawaii

Challenge

Despite travelling and competing all over the world, seven-time world champion, Layne Beachley thought Hawaii was one of the best.

A surfer being wiped out by a massive wave off the island of Maui, Hawaii

SCARY WAVES

Some professional surfers train their whole lives to surf big waves.

The scariest wave in the world is called Jaws. Jaws is located by the island of Maui in Hawaii. Jaws can break with a wave height of 24 metres (79 feet)!

Dungeons

A wave called Dungeons, near Cape Town in South Africa, is also very scary.

The break of the Dungeons wave is not as big as Jaws, but it does break between 0.5–1.5 miles (1–2 km) out to sea in freezing cold water.

You can only surf Jaws by being towed in by a jet ski

Jaws breaks over a sharp reef and ends on big cliffs with large and dangerous rocks.

SAFETY AND RULES

The powerful and changeable ocean makes surfing dangerous.

Sunset Beach, Hawaiii. The clear water in the middle of the beach is the rip going out to sea

Rips

With waves constantly pushing water to the shore, sea water needs to return back to the open ocean.

It does this by travelling through deep channels on the ocean floor. These channels are called rips, and can sweep even the strongest swimmers out to sea.

Sharks

The odds of a shark attack are fairly low, but the risks are still there.

In the 20th century, there were a total of between 30 and 75 shark attacks worldwide.

US surfer Bethany Hamilton was attacked by a shark at the age of 13 when surfing in Hawaii

Two surfers get tangled up trying to work out who has the right of way

Rules

There is an unwritten surfing code. This code says that the surfer who is already riding the wave, or who is paddling closest to the breaking part, has the right to surf that wave first.

THE BASIC MOVES

The first thing to figure out is how to stand on the board. You can either be a goofy footer or a regular (natural) footer.

A goofy surfs with the right foot forward.
A regular surfs with the left foot forward.

Paddle out

A surfer usually paddles out through the waves to the take-off zone.

Duck dive

A duck dive enables a surfer to go under an oncoming wave when paddling out.

Paddling

To get enough speed to catch a wave, it is important to do three or four quick paddling strokes just before the wave breaks.

Take-off

Professional surfers stand up at the very last second and take-off on the wave.

DIFFERENT MOVES

Once a new surfer has mastered the basics they can learn some different moves.

Tube

A tube is where a surfer is covered up by the lip of the wave and is locked inside.

Another name for a tube is a barrel.

Bottom-hand turn

This is the first move every surfer makes. The surfer leans over at the bottom of the wave after take-off and heads for the open face.

Re-entry

A basic move where the surfer turns on the top part of the wave before 're-entering' back down the face.

Cutback

After gaining speed on the open face, a surfer rides to the top of the crest. Then they cutback by turning the board toward the beach and then aiming back toward where the wave is breaking.

Aerial

This move became popular in the 1980s. The surfer and board leave the water, fly into the air and land.

KITE SURFING

The new sport of kite surfing has started to influence surfing.

Kite surfers leap into the air and perform moves up to 40 metres (130 feet) from the water's surface.

Twists

The use of a kite allows a surfer to generate more speed and to jump higher into the air.

Surfers can do more advanced twists and turns in the air.

Wind

A lot of surfers use both forms of surfing. In strong winds, they kite surf and try new tricks.

When the wind dies down, the surfers return to a normal board.

Speed

Kite-surfing experts can reach speeds of 50 miles (80 km) per hour.

A surfer rises at least 1.8 metres (6 feet) into the air above the ocean.

Taj Burrow gets ready to land. Burrow was one of the world's best aerial surfers.

AERIAL SURFING

More and more surfing is now being performed in the air above a wave, rather than on it. These moves are known as aerials. Top surfers can perform aerials 3 metres (10 feet) above the water!

2005 world champion Chelsea Georgeson gets speed to perform an aerial

Aerials involve the surfer spinning and trying to perform as many turns as possible in one go.

Complex moves such as a full somersault aren't yet possible.

A FlowRider in Malaysia

WAVE POOLS

One of the most successful wave-pool inventions is the FlowRider. The FlowRider is a standing wave that was designed by American Tom Lochtefeld.

A wave is created that stays in exactly the same position and at the same height.

Aerial specialist Josh Kerr

Surfers can perform the same turns in wave pools that they can on real waves.

HIGH WAVES

Pete Cabrinha rides Jaws, off the coast of Maui, Hawaii, which was measured at 21 metres (69 feet)

How high?

A wave is 21 metres (69 feet) high if the wave face is 21 metres high. Photographs and video footage are used to measure exactly how high the wave face is.

A surfer rides Ghost Trees in California, which is famed for its big waves

Wave waiters

There are always surfers waiting for the big waves to be discovered. The trick is finding where the waves are.

Big awards

As of 2021, the largest wave ever surfed was 24.38 metres (80 feet) high.

It was surfed by Rodrigo Koxa in 2017, off the coast of Praia do Norte, Nazaré, in Portugal.

IMPORTANT EVENTS

Surfing is recognised as an official sport and major surfing competitions are held every year in different parts of the world.

Some of these competitions include....

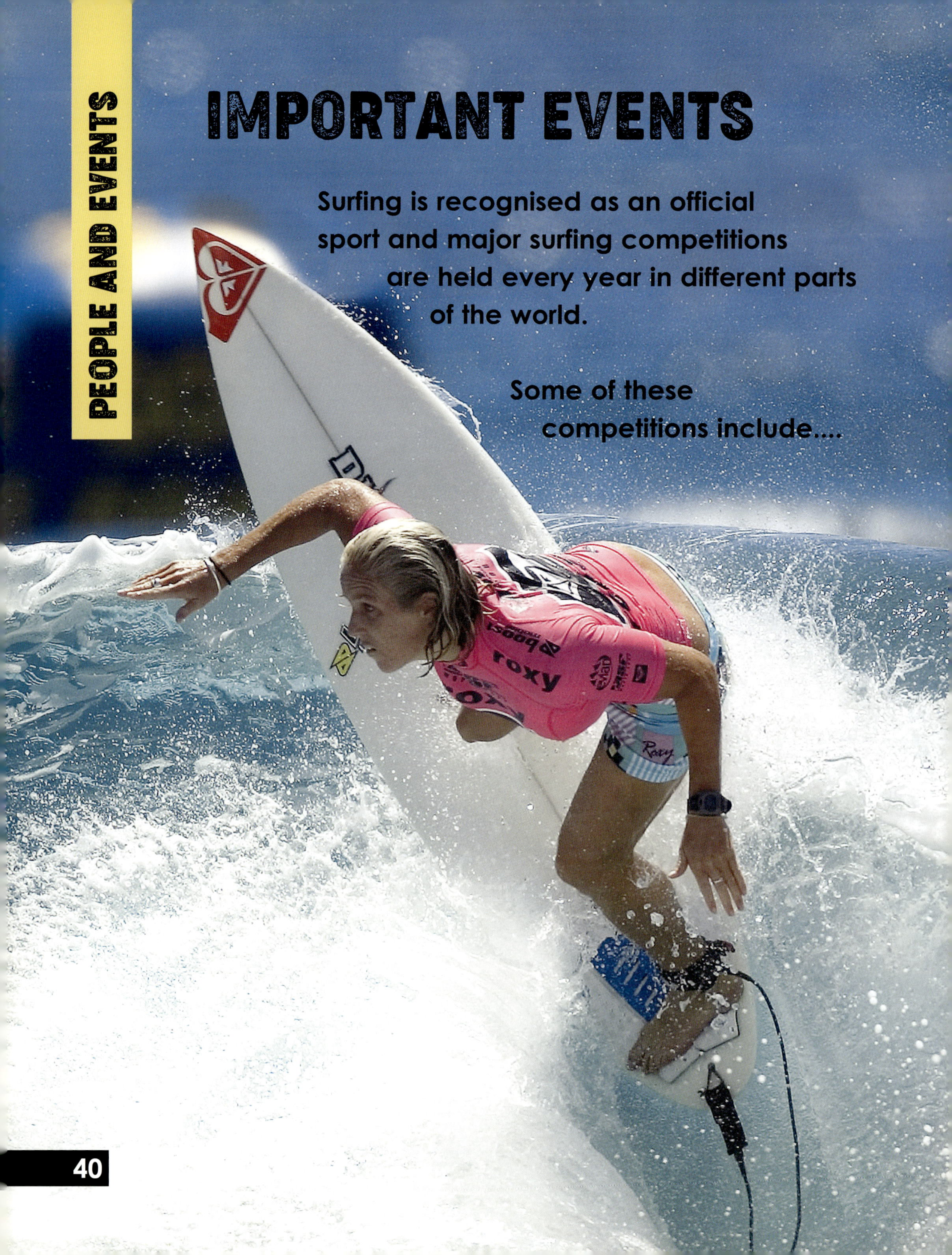

Vans Triple Crown of Surfing

Launched on 21 December 2020, the Vans Triple Crown of Surfing's official contest format transformed into an innovative, digital, free surf competition experience, due to the COVID-19 Pandemic.

ASP World Tour

Held in different locations across the world. Men and women are judged for their flow, speed, maneuvers and innovation. Scores are awarded from 0 to 10, with 10 being the best.

British Surfing Championships

An annual competition bringing together the best surfers in Britain. In Dec 2020, British surfing was awarded £1.35 million in Olympic funding.

AMAZING SURFING ACHIEVMENTS

Jordy Smith

South African, Jordy Smith has won a World Junior Championship in 2006, the World Qualifying series in 2007, and has since had several Championship Tour wins.

Adriano de Souza

This Brazilian was named the youngest-ever junior champion when he won the Junior ASP World Championship at age 16.

De Souza went on to win the WSL World Championship in 2015.

Stephanie Gilmore

This Australian won her first-ever professional event, the Quiksilver Pro, at the age of 17.

At the same age, she won her first world championship, the Roxy Pro.

Carissa Moore

American, Moore burst onto the surfing scene as a tiny 11 year old in 2002. At 14, she defeated then world champion Layne Beachley, and went on to become the 2011, 2013, 2015 and 2019 WSL Women's World Tour Champion.

MILESTONES

1912 – Hawaii's Duke Kahanamoku wins a gold medal in swimming at the Olympics. Then he travels around the world spreading the word about surfing.

1914 – The first Australian surfer, Isobel Lathem, takes to the water.

1957 – America's Greg Noll surfs Waimea surf spot in Hawaii for the first time. This is considered the start of big-wave surfing.

1966 – Australia's Nat Young wins the world title in California. He's credited with the start of the short-board evolution.

1976 – Peter Townend, from Australia, is crowned the first-ever professional world surfing champion.

1981 – In huge waves at Bells Beach, Australia, Simon Anderson wins the Rip Curl Pro on his new invention, the tri-fin surfboard.

1988 – America's Frieda Zamba sets a new world record by winning her fourth world title.

1992 – Twenty-year-old Kelly Slater is the youngest surfer ever to win a world title.

1998 – On 'Big Thursday', a group of surfers, led by America's Ken Bradshaw, tow surf into the biggest waves ever ridden until that time.

Simon Anderson riding his own invention, the tri-fin, for the first time

GLOSSARY

Big Thursday A famous day of surfing in Hawaii in 1998 when surfers rode the biggest waves (26 metres/85 feet) in the history of the sport at the time.

Face The open part of a wave that a surfer rides down.

Fibreglass The traditional material that surfboards have been made from since the 1950s.

Goofy footer A surfer that rides with their right foot forward.

Lip The falling top section of a wave.

Pipeline A famous big-wave spot in Hawaii. It is known for its massive tubes. It breaks only 30 metres (98 feet) from shore.

Reef A ridge of sharp rock or coral near the surface of the sea.

Regular footer A surfer that rides with their left foot forward.

Sets Groups of bigger waves that arrive together. Surfers will wait for the sets, as they tend to be the best quality waves.

Take-off The start of surfing a wave when a surfer paddles and is picked up by the force of the wave. Then the surfer jumps to his feet and starts the ride.

Tow surfing A relatively new form of surfing where the surfer is towed into a wave by a powered watercraft or motorised jet ski.

Tri-fin Invented by Australian surfer and surfboard maker, Simon Anderson in 1981, the tri-fin has been the dominant design in surfing ever since.

Tube The ultimate wave in surfing. The curling front part of the wave goes over the surfer, enclosing them inside the wave.

Wave pools Human-made structures that produce waves in large pools.

World junior title Currently held every year in Australia, this is for surfers under 20-years of age.

INDEX